Hope's
Broken Snow Globe

By Kelly Chang Rickert   Illustrated by Tanya Campbell

Quarantine Publications
438 S. Pasadena Avenue
Pasadena, CA 91105
www.quarantinepublications.com

Publisher's Note: This is a work of fiction. Names, characters, places and incidents are a product of the author's imagination. Locales and public names are sometimes used for atmospheric purposes. Any resemblances to actual people, living or dead, are strictly coincidental.

Ordering information: special discounts are available on quantity purchases by corporations, associations and others. For details, please contact the publisher.

Quarantine Publications - First Edition

ISBN: 978-1-7352618-4-3

Acknowledgments

So grateful for my family: Scott, Adia and Raya – I love you guys. Big shoutout to my amazing assistant Phebe and my talent illustrator Tanya, who've weathered the storms of self-publishing with me (twice!). To all my friends and family who supported my first children's book, *Two Adventures with Mom and Dad,* I gave you a fair warning this would be an annual thing! Special thanks to Stephen Eaton for your brilliant idea. And to my Heavenly Father, thank you for steering this ship back into the light – Your will be done through me on earth!

Do not be anxious about anything, but in every situation, by prayer and petition, with thanksgiving, present your requests to God. And the peace of God, which transcends all understanding, will guard your hearts and your minds in Christ Jesus.

Philippians 4:6-7 NIV

Dedication

There is a special place in my heart for the children of separation or divorce.

Because I do not get the opportunity to work with them, I write books.

To every child who has more than one home, this book is for you.

Thanksgiving was over, but Hope could still smell the pumpkin pie in her house. Very soon there would be the new scent of pine needles in the air, the smell of a Christmas tree! First though, it was time to get the decorations out from the garage.

Hope's dad came indoors with a big cardboard box, stuffed with glass ornaments, fairy lights and glittering tinsel that tumbled over the sides. Hope was so excited to get the house ready for Christmas! However, as they started to remove the decorations, she felt her excitement change into a different feeling.

Hope picked out three matching Christmas stockings. The names sewn into them were Dad, Hope and Mom. Hope felt really sad. She didn't know if Mom would be at home for Christmas.

As Dad left in his truck to pick up the tree, Hope reached the bottom of the cardboard box, where a smaller box was covered in bubble wrap.

Inside was a collection of snow globes.

There, in the center, was a single broken globe. This one no longer sparkled, its cracked glass held together by Scotch tape.

As soon as she saw it, Hope felt incredibly guilty.

As she stared at the shattered glass, Hope remembered last Christmas. She could still see the pieces of the snow globe after it smashed on the kitchen floor. She could still feel her wet feet, as the glittering water spread across the tiles. She could still hear Mom and Dad shouting in the bedroom upstairs.

Hope couldn't remember if the arguing had happened before she dropped the ornament, or after. What she did remember was, not long after the snow globe broke, her Dad moved out. Not long after that, Mom and Dad told her they were going to stop living together.

A week or so later, as Hope looked at the decorated tree, her eyes filled with tears again as she remembered last Christmas.

If she hadn't broken the snow globe, maybe her parents wouldn't have gotten divorced.

Hope had an idea! If she could fix the snow globe, maybe it would bring them back together.

Maybe Mom would come home for Christmas after all!

Excitedly but quietly, Hope snuck out of the house, carefully holding the shattered globe in a little box.

She walked briskly over the snowy ground, towards the hardware store around the corner.

At the hardware store, Old Nick the Carpenter peered at the snow globe through his little round glasses.
"I'm sorry," he said, "but there are just too many cracks to repair it. I can't make it the same as it was before. I could make you something new with the pieces. Would you like that?"

Hope felt a bit annoyed, and confused.

"No," she replied, "I need to bring my mom and dad back together. I don't want the snow globe to be different. It has to be the same. It has to be perfect!"

Old Nick stroked his bushy white beard. "If you're looking for something perfect," he said, "you'd better go to the superstore."

Hope walked a little quicker as she headed to the superstore, nearly stumbling on the slippery ground. She couldn't be gone too long, or her dad would return and notice she was missing.

At the superstore, a smiling lady listened to Hope's story.

"That's lovely sweetie," she said. "I'm sure we can help you out – No problem!"

She showed Hope to an aisle, where hundreds of snow globes rose from ceiling to floor.

"Here you are honey," said the smiling lady,

"I'm sure these are much bigger and better than what you had before!"

Hope rushed out of the superstore with a frown.

The smiling lady hadn't listened to her at all! Why had the old carpenter sent her there?

Now it was getting dark and she would have to run. Her dad would surely be angry with her when she got home.

Dashing along the snowy sidewalk, Hope sped around the corner of her street.

As she rushed up her driveway, Hope skidded and the box flew from her hands... into the air!

Hope heard a smash as the box hit the ground. She was too scared to open it. She crept back into the warm house, which smelt of gingerbread. Luckily, Dad was busy making Christmas cookies in the kitchen. He hadn't noticed Hope was gone.

In the safety of her bedroom, Hope nervously opened the box. The snow globe was still held together by the tape, but now it had so many cracks, it looked like the glass was covered by a spider's web. It was hopeless. No one could mend the globe now. She would have to hide it.

As she looked sadly into the shattered glass, Hope saw a reflection of the cross which hung on her bedroom wall. Quickly, she kneeled by the bed.

"If you are listening, God," she prayed, "I need your help. I know you are super busy, but I really want Mom and Dad to be together again by Christmas. Please help me if you can."

Later that evening, when Hope's dad came upstairs to tuck her in, he noticed the little box hidden underneath her bed.

As soon as he saw the snow globe inside, Dad remembered what happened last Christmas.

He remembered arguing upstairs with Hope's mom. He remembered hearing the sound of smashing from the kitchen below. He remembered how upset Hope had been about the broken globe.

Dad knew how to make this Christmas much happier for Hope.

He would get the snow globe fixed.

The next weekend, Dad took the box to Old Nick's hardware store. The bearded carpenter examined the ornament inside.

"Oh dear," sighed Old Nick, "this is even more broken than before."

"You've seen it before?" asked Dad, surprised.

"Yes," said Nick, "as I told your daughter, I can't make it the same as it was, but I could make something new. As for the rest of her wish, that part is up to you."

Dad was confused. What did he mean about her wish?
Suddenly, Dad understood. He remembered last Christmas again. After
hearing the smash, he ran downstairs with Hope's mom. He remembered
how worried they had both been, how much they both cared about their
daughter. "Thanks Nick," said Dad to the old carpenter, "I know what I
need to do now." As he left the store, Dad took his cell phone from his
pocket and placed a call.

It was Christmas morning! Hope awoke early. Had her prayer been answered? She raced downstairs where Dad was already waiting for her. There, underneath the tree, was a small box. Hope tore open the wrapping paper. Inside the box was...

... a piece of paper! The words on the paper read 'Please go to the
front door'.
Hope ran to the door and pulled it open. Waiting outside was Mom.
She was holding a new snow globe.

Hope was still smiling as she enjoyed a turkey dinner with Mom and Dad. "I'm so glad you rang," Mom said to Dad, "I cried at the thought of spending this first Christmas alone." Then, she held Hope's hand. "And I'm so glad that I can spend it with you."

Hope stared into the swirling globe, which perched proudly at the center of the dinner table. It wasn't exactly the same as before, but maybe something new would be okay. Though things might be different in the future, Hope knew her prayers had been answered.

ABOUT THE AUTHOR

Kelly Chang Rickert is a Christian family law attorney in Los Angeles. She is a Certified Family Law Specialist. For over 22 years, she has exclusively handled prenuptial agreements, divorce and paternity cases involving child custody and complex property division. She has authored several books and articles published by New York Times, Forbes, Wall Street Journal, and Money Magazine. She routinely appears as a family law expert on TV and Radio to comment on various family law and custody issues in celebrity cases. Her first children's book, "Two Adventures with Mom and Dad" was an Amazon best-seller and #1 New Release.

Kelly strongly discourages "scorched earth litigation" in Family Law, and in 2015, expanded her law practice to include mediation services. Kelly is a member of LACBA, ACFLS, AFCC and LACFLA, and volunteers as a Daily Settlement Officer and Judge Pro Tem.

In her spare time, Kelly enjoys nagging her husband, embarrassing her two daughters (typical Taiwanese mother), solitary hikes in Griffith Park, and worshipping God in song. Kelly writes a blog on her website, updated weekly. Follow @lawyerkelly on Instagram, TikTok, and Medium. www.purposedrivenlawyers.com

ABOUT THE ILLUSTRATOR

Tanya is a concept artist working in television and film, as well as a freelance illustrator for comics and children's books. She has been in the industry for 12 years and has worked on such productions as My Little Pony, Polly Pocket, Peabody and Sherman, Transformers Rescue Bots, with many notable clients, including Hasbro and Marvel.

Originally based out of Vancouver, Canada, Tanya has achieved most of her studio work by being a background artist for children's cartoons and television. Her home base is now Los Angeles, California, as she continues her freelance work.

Tanya draws most of her inspiration from nature, and her home Island on the coast of British Columbia. She loves creating worlds that are fun, vibrant, colorful, and bring out the kid in everyone.

You can follow more of her work on Instagram, twitter, her art blog and Facebook page.

https://www.instagram.com/tanyalehoux/
http://tanyalehoux.blogspot.com/
https://www.facebook.com/TanyaCillustration/
https://twitter.com/tanyalehoux/

Made in the USA
Columbia, SC
03 November 2021